Sly the Sleuth

and the Pet Mysteries

by Donna Jo Napoli and Robert Furrow
illustrated by Heather Maione

Dial Books for Young Readers New York

Dial Books for Young Readers
A division of Penguin Young Readers Group
Published by The Penguin Group
Penguin Group (USA) Inc., 345 Hudson Street, New York, NY 10014, U.S.A.
Penguin Group (Canada), 10 Alcorn Avenue, Toronto, Ontario, Canada M4V 3B2
(a division of Pearson Penguin Canada Inc.)
Penguin Books Ltd, 80 Strand, London WC2R 0RL, England
Penguin Ireland, 25 St. Stephen's Green, Dublin 2, Ireland
(a division of Penguin Books Ltd.)
Penguin Books India Pvt Ltd,
11 Community Centre, Panchsheel Park, New Delhi - 110 017, India
Penguin Group (NZ), Cnr Airborne and Rosedale Roads, Albany, Auckland,
New Zealand (a division of Pearson New Zealand Ltd)
Penguin Books (South Africa) (Pty) Ltd, 24 Sturdee Avenue, Rosebank,
Johannesburg 2196, South Africa
Penguin Books Ltd, Registered Offices: 80 Strand, London WC2R 0RL, England

Designed by Jasmin Rubero
Text set in Bembo
Manufactured in China

3 5 7 9 10 8 6 4 2

Library of Congress Cataloging-in-Publication Data
Napoli, Donna Jo, date.
Sly the Sleuth and the pet mysteries
by Donna Jo Napoli and Robert Furrow;
illustrated by Heather Maione.
p. cm.
Summary: Sly the Sleuth, also known as Sylvia, solves three
mysteries for her friends and neighbors, all involving pets,
through her detective agency, Sleuth for Hire.
ISBN 0-8037-2993-6
[1. Pets—Fiction. 2. Mystery and detective stories.] I. Furrow, Robert, date. II.
Maione, Heather Harms, ill. III. Title.
PZ7.N15Sl 2005
[Fic]—dc22   2003024090

*The artwork for this book was created with pen and ink.
Watercolors and colored pencils were also used
for the jacket artwork.*

To Taxi.
Love, Robert and Mamma

For my children, Luke and
Lindsay, with love
—H.M.

Case #1:
Sly and the Fat Cat

My Name

I was born Sylvia. My parents called me Sylvia. My friends called me Sylvia.

A couple of years ago a new family moved in next door. They had a son, Brian. Brian was two then. (He's four now.)

Brian couldn't say "Sylvia."

He called me Thi. Then Si. Then Sly.

I liked that. And the name stuck. Now everyone calls me Sly.

What's in a name?

Who knows.

But my friend Melody plays the piano. And my friend Jack is always jumping out of places.

And I am a sleuth.

A sleuth must sneak around. And gather clues. And be smart enough to figure out what the clues mean.

A sleuth must be sly.

I am Sly the Sleuth.

So maybe there's a lot in a name.

My Agency

I run an agency called Sleuth for Hire. I solve problems. But I am picky. I take only cases that are fun. And only cases a cat would care about.

Why?

I like cats. Cats sneak around, like sleuths.

And I have a cat. Her name is Taxi. She's my buddy. Every sleuth needs someone to talk to. Taxi is a good listener. She purrs when I tell her how I solved a case.

When I want her, I go outside and call, "Taxi, Taxi." Strangers passing on the sidewalk think I am crazy. But that's okay. It's good for business. My father says there's no such thing as bad advertising. The important thing is that people remember you.

Taking My First Case

My first case was about a fat cat. It happened just a week after I had announced the opening of my agency.

Kate stopped me on my way to the playground with Melody. "My cat is fat and getting fatter."

"So what?" I said.

"I don't want her to be fat," said Kate. "It's not good for her."

"Feed her less."

"I do," said Kate.

Melody pointed her toe. "Bring her to my house and I'll play the piano and she can dance off her fat."

"My cat's too fat to dance," said Kate. "She can hardly move."

This seemed like a pretty dumb case. I didn't want to take it.

But then Kate said, "I'm worried." She looked like she might cry. She added, "I love Clarissa."

I believed her. No one would name their cat Clarissa unless they loved her. And I understood, because I love Taxi.

"Let me think about this," I said.

Melody and Kate went on to the playground.

I went home. I stood on the front step and called, "Taxi!"

A man on the sidewalk looked at me, then looked away fast.

Taxi came running.

I rubbed her behind the ears and on her back right above her tail, which is her favorite spot.

Brian came over from next door. "Play with me."

"Not now," I said. "I'm thinking."

Brian screamed, "Think stink." He pulled Taxi's tail and ran away.

This case was about a cat. And it was about food. Taxi was a cat and Taxi loved food. So I knew Taxi would like listening to me talk about this case. Probably any cat would.

I went to the playground and found Kate.

"Okay," I said. "Take me to see Clarissa's food dish."

Clarissa

Clarissa's food dish had her name on it, drawn in big letters with a blue marker. It also had pictures of fish drawn in green marker. It was pretty. And it was empty. And clean.

"Did you wash this dish?" I asked.

"No. Clarissa always licks it clean."

Wow. Clarissa was quite a cat. The dish was perfectly clean.

"It's time for Clarissa's breakfast," said Kate. She put one-third of a can of cat food in Clarissa's dish. Then she added a small handful of crunchy, dry cat food.

"That's all?" I asked.

"Yup."

"How many times a day does she get a meal like that?"

"Breakfast and supper," said Kate.

"That's all?" I asked.

"Yup."

That was less than Taxi ate, and Taxi wasn't fat. "Clarissa should be a thin cat."

"The vet said that too," said Kate. "But see for yourself." Kate went to the window and called, "Clarissa, breakfast!"

The next thing I knew, a very large fuzzy gray head came through the middle of the rubber cat door. Clarissa looked around. "Meow," she said. Then her two front legs came through. "Meow!" she said louder. She was huge. And she was stuck.

Kate grabbed Clarissa's front legs and gently pulled her inside.

Clarissa was the fattest cat I'd ever seen. And she didn't have a collar. People who love their cats put collars on them. "Why don't you have a collar on your cat?"

"It pops off," said Kate.

"How can a collar pop off?"

Kate opened a drawer and took out a collar.

Clarissa was eating away happily.

Kate put the collar on Clarissa. Clarissa's neck was so big, the collar barely made it around.

As soon as it was on, Clarissa stopped eating. She worked her front paw under the collar. The clasp gave and the collar popped off. Clarissa went back to eating.

Easy Answers

Clarissa ate every morsel in her dish. She licked the plate. Then she sat and cleaned her paws and face.

Kate petted Clarissa tenderly.

"Clarissa is even fatter now than she was when she came in," I said. "How will she get out her cat door?"

Kate opened the people door and Clarissa waddled outside. "Can you help me figure out what's making Clarissa so fat?"

"Maybe she's going to have kittens," I said.

"The vet said she can't," said Kate.

Oh, well. So much for easy answers.

We stood side by side and watched Clarissa lie down in the sun.

A couple of sparrows hopped about in a bush.

I got an idea. It was a long shot, but it was worth a try. "Do you have stale bread?" I asked.

"What?" said Kate.

"You know, bread to feed birds. Got any?"

"Sure." Kate opened a bag on the counter. She handed me a piece of old bread.

I crushed it in my hand and threw the bread crumbs on the ground near Clarissa.

Clarissa looked, but she didn't move.

The sparrows flew down and ate the crumbs.

Clarissa watched them. Then she rolled onto her back.

"Well, your cat didn't get fat eating birds," I said. "I bet she'd be too slow to catch them even if she tried."

"Poor Clarissa," said Kate.

The Search for Clues

Clarissa slept.

While she slept, I went around the yard looking for clues.

Kate followed me. "What are you doing?"

"Looking for clues."

"Like what?"

"I don't know."

"What good is it to keep looking, then?"

This was not an encouraging question to hear on my first case. I held my head high. "That's what sleuths do," I said.

"That seems dumb to me," said Kate.

"Do you want Clarissa to lose weight or not?" I asked, which was not a fair question for two reasons. First, I knew the answer. Second, I wasn't sure I could help make Clarissa lose weight.

"I do," said Kate.

"Are you hiring me or not?"

"I am," said Kate.

"Then go away."

Kate went into her house.

I looked harder for clues. I found none.

Clarissa woke up. She walked slowly to the bushes and disappeared under them.

I followed her.

Another Fat Cat

Clarissa was not under the bushes.

I crawled through and watched Clarissa cross the backyard of Kate's neighbor.

Maybe Clarissa was a friendly cat who visited the neighbors for fun.

But Clarissa kept on going. She came to a hole in the fence and struggled through to the second neighbor.

The hole was large enough that I could get through just by holding my breath. I could see why Kate was worried. Clarissa sure was a fat cat.

By the time I got out on the other side, Clarissa was nowhere in sight.

I walked around the fence, looking for another hole. There wasn't one.

Clarissa had disappeared.

"Boo!"

I jumped.

But it was just my friend Jack, jumping at me.

"What are you doing here?" I asked Jack.

"This is my yard. What are you doing here?"

"Oh, I didn't recognize your house from the back."

"You didn't answer me," said Jack.

"I'm being Sly the Sleuth today. And I'm looking for Clarissa."

"You're not supposed to go in other people's yards unless they invite you. Didn't anyone ever tell you that? And there's no Clarissa here."

"Did you see a fat cat?"

"Of course I saw a fat cat," said Jack. "That's my cat."

"Your cat is fat?" I said. Maybe it was something in the water on this block.

"I think she looks tough," said Jack.

"That's fine with me," I said. "Could I meet her?"

"She's eating, and she doesn't like to be bothered when she's eating. Then she'll nap. And she doesn't like to be bothered when she's napping either."

"I'll wait," I said.

"Good. You can practice passing the soccer ball with me."

"Uh, I play baseball. I stink at soccer. I'll go wait on the front sidewalk," I said.

All Cats Do

"What are you doing sitting on the sidewalk?" It was Kate. She was standing over me. "You're supposed to be working."

"We never talked about my fee," I said.

"What is it?"

Since this was my first case, I had no idea. "The usual," I said.

Kate blinked. "Will two doll dresses be enough?"

"I don't like dolls," I said. "I don't even have any."

"Well, that's what I have."

I could always trade doll dresses for something better. "Okay," I said.

"So get up and work," said Kate.

"I am working," I said. "Do you drink the same water that Clarissa drinks?"

"Sure," said Kate. "Except she also drinks from rain puddles, and I don't."

Kate was thin. So that ruled out the idea that the water was the cause.

"Get up and work," said Kate. Boy, she could be bossy.

"I happen to be working very hard," I said. "I'm tracking Clarissa."

"Well, if you're tracking her, you better go before she gets out of sight."

"What?" I looked where Kate pointed. There was Clarissa, trotting slowly along the sidewalk toward the corner. "Does your cat wander a lot?"

"Of course," said Kate. "All cats do."

I didn't know if that was true. Taxi always came when I called. But maybe she knew when I wouldn't call her and that's when she wandered. Maybe she wandered far when I was at school or sleeping. "Bye," I said. I followed Clarissa.

Two Too Many

Clarissa turned the corner and cut into someone's yard. She went around the side of their house.

I remembered what Jack had said about going into other people's yards. But what choice did I have? I followed Clarissa.

When I got to the side of the house, she was gone.

I ran to the backyard.

No Clarissa.

I could see a woman standing at her kitchen sink. I went up and knocked on the side door.

The woman opened the door. "Yes?"

"I'm looking for a fat cat."

"My cat is slightly overweight," said the woman with a sniff. "But I wouldn't call her fat."

"You have a fat cat?" I practically yelped. This was remarkable.

"I told you that's not the word I would use. Although I admit that's what our vet's assistant said."

Now I was totally suspicious. Three fat cats was two too many. "Is her name Clarissa?"

"No. She's Punky."

Punky was not half bad for a cat's name. This woman surprised me.

"Is she gray?"

"Yes."

"I've got it," I said. "Please bring your cat to Kate's house."

"I beg your pardon," she said. "I don't know who or what you're talking about."

"Kate has something in common with you, and she lives in the green house around the corner. Be there in fifteen minutes, please. It's important. Please? Bye."

Getting It Together

I ran back around the corner and stopped at Jack's house. I rang the doorbell.

When he opened the door, he said, "You're too late. My cat went out already."

"I know," I said.

"Oh. Did you change your mind about soccer?"

"No."

"Then why are you here?" said Jack.

"You have to come to a meeting at Kate's house in ten minutes."

"Kate? Why? She's so bossy."

"She's all right," I said.

Jack made a face. "What's this all about?"

"Something important. Be there. Bye." I ran to Kate's house.

She was waiting for me on the front steps. "Did you follow Clarissa?"

"Yes," I said.

"So where is she?"

"She'll be here in a few minutes," I said. "Have you got any cookies and milk?"

"Cookies and milk are the last thing Clarissa needs," said Kate.

"Right. But they're exactly what the people will need."

"What people?" said Kate.

"You'll see. They'll be here soon. And they'll need a treat."

"I thought you liked fruit," said Kate.

"I do." I'm a fruit fiend.

"Then everyone else gets cookies and you get cherries."

Sometimes I'm glad Kate's bossy.

Sharing

The woman showed up with Clarissa in her arms. I knew she would.

"Why are you holding Clarissa?" said Kate.

"Why are you holding Fluffy?" said Jack.

"This is Punky," said the woman.

Kate's mother came down the stairs. "I thought I heard an adult's voice. Hello." She held out her hand to the woman. "I'm Sarah, Kate's mother."

The woman looked at Kate's mother's hand. She couldn't shake without putting Clarissa down. She blinked. "I'm Julie. I live around the corner. That child . . ." She looked at me. "That child told me to come here with my cat."

"Your cat?" said Kate's mother. She peeked behind the woman. "Where's your cat?"

"This is my cat," said the woman named Julie.

"No it's not," said Kate. "Mother, make her put Clarissa down."

Kate bossed her mother like that a lot. And her mother usually let her get away with it.

"Well, now," Kate's mother said in a reasonable tone. "There's some mistake here. That's Clarissa."

"This is Punky," said the woman named Julie. She didn't sound at all reasonable. She sounded like Kate.

"Everyone please sit down and have cookies and milk," I said.

"I don't eat cookies and milk," said the woman named Julie.

Jack jumped beside me and took the dish. "I'll eat them all."

Clarissa looked at the milk. "Meow," she said.

"This is why your cat is so fat," I said. "She has convinced all of you that she belongs to you.

And all of you feed her. So she gets a lot more food than she needs."

"But she's mine," said Kate. "I got her when she was just a kitten. Tell them, Mother."

"No, she's mine," said the woman named Julie. "I paid for her to get fixed."

"So that's why she can't have babies," said Kate.

"She's mine," said Jack.

We all looked at him to hear his reason. But he just stuffed another cookie in his mouth.

"Put my cat down right now," said Kate.

"Kate," said Kate's mother, "you don't have to be rude." She looked at the woman named Julie. "We need to talk. Why don't you put Clarissa down and have a seat?"

"I don't think so. I'm taking her home," said the woman named Julie.

"No you don't," said Jack. "Give her to me."

"Wait," I said. "This can work out. Listen. You've all been happy with this cat so far, right?"

"Right," they said together.

"So you can continue sharing her. You just have

to agree to cut back on how much you feed her."

They were quiet for a minute.

"That'll save me some money," said Jack.

"And we can take turns bringing her to the vet," said Kate's mother. She tilted her head at the woman named Julie. "That will save even more money."

"True," said the woman named Julie. She squatted and slowly set Clarissa on the floor.

We all looked at Kate.

"All right," she said finally.

The Trade

So my first case ended in success. And Taxi purred the whole time I told her about it.

That was two months ago. Clarissa-Fluffy-Punky is now a little thinner. And no one has complained. I introduced her to Taxi and they play sometimes. And she now has a much sturdier

collar that she can't pop off, with three phone numbers on one side and *C-F-P* on the other.

Kate's mother and the woman named Julie have become sort of friends. They jogged together a few times, until Julie hurt her knee. Now they lift weights in Kate's basement on Saturday mornings.

I traded the two doll dresses for some baseball cards. That was with Melody. I hadn't even known she collected them before. It's funny what you don't know about the people around you.

Case #2:
Sly and the Wish Fish

The Monster

I came home from school on Friday and headed for the backyard hammock.

Brian came over from next door. "Are you tired?"

"Yes," I said.

"Because you had a rough day at school?"

"Yes," I said, although it wasn't a particularly rough day. But with Brian it's best to keep answers short.

"My day was rough too," said Brian.

"How could nursery school be rough?" I said. But I knew right away that was a bad question.

For one, Brian would answer. So that meant he would stay awhile. For another, I remembered nursery school. Nursery school had some pretty rough days.

"A monster came to our classroom," said Brian.

"Sure, Brian," I said.

"It did. A real monster," said Brian. "Can I come into the hammock with you?"

"Why?" I asked.

Brian climbed in beside me. "I'm scared."

I thought about pushing him out. But he did look scared. And people my age shouldn't push four-year-olds. "Why are you scared?"

"He followed me home. He's a bad monster."

I decided to approach this rationally, which had never worked with Brian before, but there was always a first time. "Don't you drive home?" I asked.

"Monsters can follow cars," said Brian.

"How do you know?"

"Because there he is."

Blue

"Boo!"

Brian screamed and threw himself on me.

I pressed down Brian's shoulder so I could see over it. "Hi, Jack."

"How did you know it was me?" said Jack.

"Jack?" Brian held on to me tight and peeked

around at Jack. "You know a monster by name?"

"He's not a monster," I said. "Monsters don't say 'Boo.'"

"What do monsters say?" said Brian.

"Yeah?" said Jack.

"They roar."

Jack roared.

Brian screamed.

"Cut it out," I said to both of them. "Anyway, monsters aren't blue."

"That's what you think," said Jack.

I examined Jack from head to foot. All his clothes were blue, even his socks. His hair was

dyed blue. His hands were blue. Then I got it.
"Why are you dressed like Cookie Monster?"

"This is my Halloween costume."

"Halloween isn't till Sunday," I said.

"My class did a parade for the nursery school,"
said Jack.

"See?" I said to Brian. "There's a simple expla-
nation. Jack is just playing Cookie Monster."

"Who's Cookie Monster?" said Brian.

I forgot. Brian's mother doesn't have a TV. And
she doesn't let him eat junk food. Her usual snack
for him is flaxseed sprinkled on prunes. The only
cookies she ever serves come from the health food
store. They taste like dry cat food. The last time
she gave me one, I fed it to Taxi. "Cookie Monster
is not someone to worry about," I said.

"That's not true," said Jack. "I come into people's
houses and eat all their cookies."

I whispered to Jack, "You don't want the cookies
in Brian's house." Then I said in a regular voice,
"He won't go into your house, Brian. So what are
you doing here, Jack?"

"I have a problem," said Jack. "It's a mystery."

"I'm Sly the Sleuth," I said quickly. "I run Sleuth for Hire."

"I know."

"Did you come to hire me?"

"If you can solve my problem."

"What's your problem?" I said.

"My fish hates me."

This sounded kind of wacky, even for Jack. "Go on," I said.

Wish Fish

Jack sat down beside me. Three people on our hammock is a lot. It sagged so much, Brian and I tumbled against Jack.

Brian screamed.

"Cut it out," I said. "No more screaming. This is just Jack."

"And I'm sad," said Jack. "No one should be afraid of a sad monster."

"Start at the beginning," I said. That was a line my mother told me detectives always say.

"For my birthday I wished for a fish."

"I wish for fish every day," said Brian.

We both looked at Brian. Maybe it was time to send him home.

"Why would you wish for a fish?" I asked Jack. "You already have a cat."

"I like fish," said Jack. "So my mother bought me Wish Fish. And he loved me."

"How do you know?" I asked.

"Well, maybe he didn't love me," said Jack. "But he didn't hate me. He ignored me. He stayed in his bowl happy as a clam."

"Are clams happy?" said Brian.

He had a point. Why did people always say clams were happy? Maybe they were depressed. They never did anything fun, after all.

"I don't know," said Jack, "but Wish Fish was happy."

"How do you know?" said Brian.

"Leave the questions to me," I said to Brian. "How do you know, Jack?"

"He ate and swam," said Jack.

That seemed as good a piece of evidence as any.

"So what happened?" I asked.

"It started last night. I stopped by Wish Fish's bowl and he got mad."

A mad fish? "How could you tell?"

"I just could. And this morning before school he got mad again. Even madder than last night."

I had to see this fish for myself.

But first, I had to decide: Did I want to take the case?

"Taxi," I called.

Taxi came running.

"How come your cat always comes when you call?" said Jack. "Ordinary cats only come at meal-time."

"Taxi's not ordinary," I said.

I moved Brian to one side and scooped up Taxi. I rubbed my chin on the top of her head. She liked that.

This case was about a fish. Taxi loved to eat fish. And this was a mad fish. Taxi almost never got mad. She'd want to know why a fish was mad. Probably any cat would.

"Take me to Wish Fish," I said.

Mad

Brian went home.

Jack and I walked to his house.

"Well, hello, Sly," said Jack's mother. "I haven't seen you for a while."

"Hello, Mrs. Carver. I came to see Jack's fish."

"How nice. When you're done, come have a snack." Mrs. Carver went into the kitchen. I was glad. Mrs. Carver made good snacks, like yummy fruit pies. It was too bad Brian couldn't have come with us. He could use some real treats.

"This way," said Jack. He led me to his room. He stopped in the doorway and pointed.

I looked across the clutter to the fishbowl. It sat on top of a low bureau. The fish inside amazed me.

Wish Fish had a filmy tail that was wider than

his body and almost as long. He had three fins: a wide one on his back, a gigantic one on his belly, and a narrow one under his chin that streamed down to two points. All the fins were filmy and long, like that tail. When he turned, his tail and fins flowed around him. It was as though he was dancing in a gauzy veil.

Best of all, he was glowing scarlet.

Wish Fish was beautiful.

I put my face close to his bowl.

Wish Fish glided past.

I tapped on the side of the bowl.

Wish Fish blew a bubble and kept on gliding.

"He doesn't look mad," I said.

"Watch." Jack walked up to the bowl and put his face close.

Wish Fish jerked to attention. He faced Jack. He spread his fins and gill covers. He wiggled fast. I had to admit he looked mad. He looked ferocious.

"He only hates me," said Jack. He slumped down onto the floor. "Only me."

Dirty Water

"Fish aren't smart enough to hate a particular person," I said.

Jack didn't look convinced.

"Listen, I once read that goldfish are so stupid, by the time they swim to one side of their bowl, they forget what's on the other side."

Jack shook his head. "Wish Fish isn't a goldfish. Mom said he's a betta."

"Fish are idiots, Jack. All fish."

"Really? Then I got the only fish in the world smart enough to hate me," moaned Jack.

I sat on the floor beside Jack. "You must have done something bad to him."

"Nothing," said Jack. "I swear. I feed him. And I even sing to him every night."

"Let me hear you sing."

"No," said Jack.

Well, that was okay. I wouldn't sing if someone asked me to either. Besides, if Jack sang every night and Wish Fish started getting mad only last night, then it couldn't be Jack's singing.

"Is there anything different you've done to him?"

"No."

I looked up at Wish Fish. The water in his bowl was scuzzy. "When did you last change his water?"

"Two weeks ago."

"Hmmm," I said. "Maybe he's a genius fish and he knows you're the one who's supposed to change his water and he wants it clean." Actually, I hated saying that, it sounded so dumb. But, after all, there weren't many things that must matter to a fish, and water's got to be among them.

"Nah. The pet store told Mom not to change his water too often. He likes dirty water. In the wild, he lives in stagnant water."

"Yuck," I said.

"Yup," said Jack. "See? Wish Fish is a perfect fish. And he hates me."

Telephone

I went home and telephoned my best friend, Melody.

No one answered.

So I telephoned Kate.

"Hello," said Kate.

"This is Sly. Want to go walk to the pet store with me?"

"I don't need a pet," said Kate. "I have Clarissa."

"I just want to look at fish," I said.

"Fish are boring," said Kate. "Look at kittens instead."

"Do you want to come with me or not?" I asked.

"Be outside my house in five minutes." Kate hung up.

The phone rang.

"Hello," I said.

"It's me," said Melody. "Let's play."

"I'm going to the pet store with Kate."

"Oh," said Melody. She didn't sound happy.

"What do you know about fish?" I asked.

"They don't taste good," said Melody.

"I mean pet store fish."

"Oh." Melody giggled. "I guess most people don't eat their pets."

I laughed too. "What do you know about red fish?"

"Red fish, blue fish, old fish, new fish," said Melody, with another giggle. "Only tropical fish come in bright colors like red."

I knew that, of course, but I was glad Melody reminded me. "Come with us," I said. "We're going to look at fish. Or I am, at least. Kate's going to look at kittens."

"Why are you looking at fish?"

"I have a case to solve."

"Goodie. I'll look at fish with you," said Melody. "I'm your best friend, after all."

The Pet Store

The kittens were in one window. Kate went to them.

The puppies were in the other window. Melody

went to them. She said they were "darling." I didn't have the heart to remind her she had promised to look at fish with me.

Oh, well, I was the sleuth, after all. And Jack had hired me, not Melody.

I got to work.

The fish tanks ran in three aisles. I started at the first one, thinking if they were alphabetical, then bettas would be near the start.

The tanks weren't alphabetical.

So I walked along looking for red fish.

I saw orange swordtails. I saw orange and black clown fish. I saw fancy goldfish that were silvery red. And I saw fancy guppies that were see-through with red insides.

But I didn't see a single glowing scarlet fish.

I started over. I read the labels on the tanks. No label said "Bettas."

This was getting nowhere.

I went to the clerk. "Excuse me," I said. "I'm Sly the Sleuth. And I'm on a case."

The clerk looked down his long nose at me. "Yes?"

"I can't find your tank of bettas."

"We don't have one," said the clerk.

"Oh. Then I guess I'll have to get my mother to drive me to another store."

"Go ahead," said the clerk. "But you won't find one."

I blinked at him. He didn't seem rude. "Why not?"

"No store has a tank of bettas," said the clerk.

Was this a trick?

So Many Bettas

"How do you know?" I asked. I used my most polite voice. After all, this clerk seemed loopy, and I didn't know what he'd do next. "How do you know no store has a tank of bettas?"

"If they did, they'd all be dead. Except maybe one." The clerk came around from the counter. "Want to know why?"

Of course I did. But the way he was acting, I wasn't about to ask.

"Why?" said Melody. She was standing behind me. Good old Melody.

"Come see." The clerk led the way to the far side of the store.

On a counter were many small bowls. Each bowl held a fish. Blue fish and purple fish and red fish and green fish.

"They're beautiful," said Melody.

"Those are bettas," said the clerk.

"Why aren't they in a tank?" asked Melody.

"A sleuth can figure it out," said the clerk. He flipped over a sign on the counter. "No cheating," he said with a wink. Then he left us there.

"You shouldn't have said you were a sleuth," said Melody.

Well, I knew that.

"I wonder what that sign says," said Melody. "I suppose it would be cheating to turn it over."

"Yup," I said.

"What are you going to do, then?" asked Melody.

I didn't know. And her question didn't help.

"Go back to the puppies."

"I can't. A woman's cleaning out the window. So she put all the puppies away somewhere."

"There are parakeets in the back of the store," I said.

"I like birds."

"Go see them," I said. "I won't mind."

"All right. But I'll come back soon. After all, I promised."

"Take your time," I said.

The Sign

I looked at the prettiest red betta. He was all puffed out, like Wish Fish. He was mad.

I looked at the next red fish. He was mad too.

All the red fish were mad.

And the blue. And the purple. And the green.

What a bunch of mad fish.

What was wrong with them?

I looked around. No one was nearby. And these bowls were very small. I could pick them up easily.

I held one up to my face to get a good look.

The fish stopped being mad. Just like that. He closed his gill covers. He relaxed his fins. He swam in a circle.

I put the bowl down.

He got mad.

I picked up a second bowl. That fish stopped being mad too. But when I put the bowl back down, he got mad again.

Who ever heard of fish who wanted to be held?

I picked up a bowl and walked to the back of the store to find Melody.

She spied me right away. "Isn't the yellow one cute? He's sick, so they put him in a cage all alone."

The parakeet didn't look sick. He was chattering at himself in a mirror.

"I guess they put the mirror there to keep him company," said Melody.

Company. Maybe these fish were mad because they wanted company. Maybe that's why they liked being in my hands.

I held the bowl up to the side of the birdcage, so that the fish could see himself in the mirror.

He got mad.

Wow.

I ran back to the counter and picked up another bowl. With a bowl in each hand, I brought the two fish near each other.

They got mad.

I put my head down between them.

They stopped being mad.

I picked up a bowl with a red fish and a bowl with a blue fish. I held them so they could see each other. They got mad.

These fish didn't want company.

And now I knew why they weren't in tanks.

I turned over the sign. Yup, that made sense. It said: "Siamese Fighting Fish (Bettas)."

Hair Dye

I ran to the drugstore. Kate and Melody lagged behind.

"Slow down," called Kate.

"Catch up," I called back.

I went to the hair dye section. There were fourteen shades of brown. "Which one matches Jack's natural color?" I asked.

"I like his hair blue," said Melody. "He looked good at recess."

"Besides," said Kate, "you don't have any right to tell Jack what color his hair should be."

I stared at Kate. She was the one who told people what to do. But I didn't point that out. "He needs to go back to brown," I said. I chose a medium brown.

"I'd like to be a redhead," said Melody. She picked up a package. "I wonder if my mother would let me."

"Don't ask her," said Kate. She picked up a package of purple hair dye. "What about you, Sly?"

"I have to keep my mind on business," I said. "Let's go."

We bought hair dye and ran to Jack's house. I rang the bell.

Jack opened the door. "What are you all doing here?"

"We're going to have a hair-dyeing party," said Kate.

"Not at my house," said Jack.

"But you need to dye your hair brown," I said. "And you need to change your clothes."

"Why?"

"When did you dye your hair blue?" I asked.

"Last night, before I went to bed."

"And when did you put on all your blue clothes?" I asked.

"This morning."

"Exactly," I said. "Wish Fish is a Siamese Fighting Fish. They come in all colors, including blue. Last night, when you had blue hair, he suspected you were a betta too. So he got mad. Then, when you put on all blue clothes, he was sure. So he got madder. He wanted to fight you."

"I'm not a fish," said Jack.

"Wish Fish is stupid," I said. "So you have to change back to your normal colors."

"Oh." Jack smiled. "I can do that. After Halloween. In the meantime, I'll ask my mom to feed Wish Fish."

"Case solved," I said.

"Pay her," said Melody.

"What do you want?" asked Jack.

I didn't know yet. "I'll send you a bill."

Payment

Kate's house was only two doors down from Jack's. So we went there.

We also went there because Kate's mother lets her do almost anything she wants. And Kate's mother is always reasonable, so other people tend to agree with her. She called Melody's mother and got her to agree.

Kate and Melody dyed their hair.

I sat on the back steps and waited. I felt kind of left out.

Clarissa, the semi-fat cat, rubbed against my legs. She was a pretty good cat. Not extraordinary, like Taxi. But okay.

Clarissa purred.

I petted her.

I thought about Jack's question: What did I want for payment? I couldn't ask for money because Jack never had any.

I remembered the clutter in Jack's room. I couldn't ask for anything Jack had because I didn't like the things Jack had.

So what could I ask for?

Maybe I could make him my slave for a day. That wasn't a bad idea. If Jack knew how to do anything useful. But maybe he didn't.

"Boo." It was Jack, of course.

"How did you find me?"

"I watched when you left my house." Jack reached into his pocket. "Here."

It was a half-used package of blue hair dye. "What for?"

"My hair's short, so I only used half. I was saving the rest for next Halloween. But I've decided to be a pirate next Halloween."

"So how come I get it?"

"It's your payment." Jack twisted his mouth. "It's enough, isn't it?"

I looked at Jack's blue hair. Melody was right; it was a great color. "Sure. Thanks."

Halloween

It's the day after Halloween. Jack came to school with brown hair. He told me Wish Fish was happy.

I went to school with blue hair. That was not easy. Kate's mother had to talk to my mother for a long time before she agreed.

Now I'm sitting in the hammock with Taxi. We went trick-or-treating together. I was Marge Simpson. Bart's mother. She has beautiful blue hair.

Taxi was my cat.

Melody and her new puppy went with us. Melody went as a mother dog and her puppy was her baby.

This was a good second case. Daddy says I'm

honing my skills as a sleuth. But I might take a vacation from sleuthing till this dye wears off. Blue hair makes me stand out. And a sleuth needs to be able to go unnoticed.

Case #3:
Sly and the Third Case

Tears

I sat on the back stoop. It was one of those warm days that comes like a surprise in the middle of November. A good day to do homework outside.

I took out my spelling list.

"Catch Taxi," screamed Brian. He ran over from next door.

"Why?" I said.

Brian screamed again. "Catch her, fast."

"Taxi," I called.

Taxi came running.

"Hold her," screamed Brian.

I pulled Taxi onto my lap.

"Lock her up," screamed Brian.

"What's this all about?" I said. "And stop screaming."

Brian sat down beside me. "Wilson got loose."

"Wilson?" Then I remembered. Brian's mother told me she was going to get him a mouse. "Is that what you named your new pet?"

"A ball knocked over the bucket," said Brian. "Lock Taxi up."

"Let me get this straight. You put Wilson in a bucket?"

Brian shook his head. "My mother did. She was cleaning Wilson's home."

What mother would put a mouse in a bucket? But, then, what mother besides Brian's would think flaxseed sprinkled on prunes was a treat? "Okay. Then a ball knocked over the bucket?"

"Taxi will kill Wilson. Lock her up."

"When did this happen?"

"After dinner."

"After dinner yesterday? Brian, if Taxi was going to kill Wilson, she's already done it."

Brian's eyes teared up. "Oh no," he sobbed. "Oh no, oh no."

I put my arm around him. "I said 'if.' Maybe Wilson is fine."

"Sly," came Melody's voice. "Oh, Sly."

I looked up.

Melody stood in the driveway. She was crying.

"What's wrong?"

"I think my puppy's dying."

Crazy

I hugged Melody.

Taxi ran into the bushes.

Brian screamed, "Catch Taxi. Catch Taxi. Catch Taxi."

"Wait a minute, Melody," I said.

I reached under the bushes. I pulled out Taxi and put her inside. "Stop screaming, Brian."

"Okay," said Brian.

I went back to Melody. "What happened?"

"He got sick."

"How awful. Did you take him to the vet?"

"No. My parents said he's fine."

This was odd. "Let's sit down."

We sat on the stoop.

Brian went over to his yard. He crawled on all fours in the grass.

"Why's Brian crawling?" asked Melody.

"Maybe he's looking for Wilson," I said. "Or maybe he's crazy."

"Who's Wilson?"

I didn't want to talk about a mouse that was probably dead. "It doesn't matter. Brian is definitely crazy."

"Maybe my puppy's crazy too," said Melody.

"Tell me about it," I said.

"Oh, good," said Melody. "I knew you'd solve my case. You said you were taking a vacation from sleuthing. But I just knew you'd come back for me."

I hadn't realized this was a case.

Did I want a new case?

My first case was about Fat Cat. My second case was about Wish Fish.

Fat Cat. Wish Fish. They rhymed.

So my third case should rhyme too. After all, things came in threes.

"Sick Puppy" didn't rhyme. "Crazy Puppy" didn't rhyme.

But this was a case about a pet. And so were the first two. So that was good.

And my hair was back to brown. As it turned out, the blue washed out in two weeks. That was the kind of dye Jack's mother had let him buy—short-term. So I could sleuth again unnoticed.

And even though Taxi didn't like dogs, she'd be interested in a sick one. Probably any cat would. So this was a case a cat would enjoy hearing me talk about.

And, most of all, this was Melody. My best friend.

"Start at the beginning," I said.

Night and Day

"Last night I took Pong outside to play."

Pong? "I thought his name was Brownie. When did you change it?"

"The other day," said Melody. "I was playing Ping-Pong and he loved it."

"I hate that game," said Brian. He had come back into my yard. "It's hard." He sprinkled grass over us.

Melody stood up. She shook off the grass.

"Pong loved it. He chased the balls. He even ate one. So I changed his name."

"If he ate a Ping-Pong ball, that's why he's sick," I said.

"No, he passed it."

I thought about that. "Eww."

"He crunched it up before he swallowed it," said Melody. "And that was days ago, anyway."

"All right," I said. "What happened last night?"

"We were playing catch."

"I like catch," said Brian. He threw another handful of grass on us.

"And he got sick," said Melody. She brushed off the grass.

"How do you mean?"

"He moved all jerky. All over the place."

"He's a puppy," I said. "That's what puppies do."

"But this was different. I ran inside and told Daddy. He put Pong to bed. And he said not to worry." Melody shrugged. "So I went to bed too."

"Did he sleep okay?"

"I guess so. He was okay this morning. I went

to school. But when I got home, he did that weird jerky stuff again. I picked him up. And he flipped out of my arms."

"Did you tell your parents?"

"They're not home. And Sharee said it was no big deal."

Sharee was Melody's after-school sitter. She said everything was no big deal.

"So you came over here," I said.

"Sharee let me. I didn't know what else to do." Melody hugged herself. "Maybe he goes crazy as the day goes on. Maybe he'll get worse and worse."

"At night he'll be really bad," said Brian.

"Hush, Brian," I said.

"He's a werewolf," said Brian.

"Dogs don't become werewolves," I said. "Only people do that."

"Maybe Pong is people really," said Brian.

"Go home, Brian," I said. "Okay, Melody, let's go see Pong."

Normal

We walked through Brian's backyard, cut through the hedge at the rear, and went into Melody's yard.

Melody opened her back door.

Pong jumped up on her.

She got on her knees. She scratched him.

"Shut the door," called Sharee. She was probably in the living room reading. That's what she always did. "And hi, Sly, come on in." I don't know how she knew I was there.

I came inside.

Pong jumped on me.

I got on my knees too.

"He seems normal," I said. I petted his soft ears.

"Now. But he went nuts a little while ago."

I looked Pong over. "What were you doing when he went nuts?"

"Playing catch."

And she was playing catch last night, when Pong first went nuts. "Play catch now," I said.

Melody went into her bedroom.

Pong followed her.

She came back with a stuffed cat.

Pong ripped it out of her hand. He ran around the room. He shook the cat in his teeth.

I thought of Taxi. "You're teaching him to bite cats," I said.

"Oh. I didn't think of that." Melody wrestled the cat away from Pong.

Pong yipped.

"He's acting normal," I said.

"But he wasn't before. Really."

"Show me what he did," I said. "Maybe then he'll do it again."

Melody squatted. Then she jumped. Then she squatted. Then she jumped in the other direction.

Pong ran around her. He leaped at her. But he didn't do what she did. "He's normal," I said.

"Stop saying that." Melody stood up. "Pong is sick."

"He doesn't act sick," I said.

"Maybe he won't do it in front of anyone else."

"I have homework," I said. I went to the door.

"But I hired you," said Melody.

"I need to think now. That's part of the job. Call me if he acts weird again."

No Good

I sat on the back stoop with a notebook and a dictionary.

Taxi pushed her head into my side. She was still mad at me for leaving her in the house.

I put my hand over her face and mushed her. It sounds bad. But I did it gentle. She loves it.

I had twenty spelling words. I had to use each one in a sentence. The first one was *evolve*. I opened the dictionary. *Evolve* means to develop. I wrote my first sentence: *My father is a photographer, so he evolves his own pictures.*

It wasn't true. My father has his pictures developed at the drugstore. But it was the best sentence I could think of.

I did the next six words just as fast.

"You're no good." Brian stood beside me.

"Don't bother me now," I said. "I have home-work."

"You let Taxi out," said Brian. He pointed a finger at Taxi.

Taxi was now resting in the dirt.

"Wilson killer," he screamed at her. "Murderer."

"You don't know for sure that Taxi killed Wilson," I said.

Brian walked over to Taxi. He grabbed her head and tried to pull open her jaw.

Taxi screeched and ran away.

"See?" said Brian. "She killed Wilson."

"How do you know?"

"She ran away," said Brian. "She's guilty."

Brian knew nothing about anything.

"Come on, Brian. Wilson might be happily digging a tunnel under your grass right now." It was possible, anyway.

"Wilson would hate tunnels," said Brian. "I do. They scare me. Wilson would like ponds. But we don't have a pond in our yard."

A mouse in a pond? But what was the point of arguing. "Maybe Wilson didn't stay in your yard," I said.

"You just want to pretend you have a good cat. But you don't," said Brian. "Your cat's no good. And you're no good."

"Bye, Brian." I picked up my things and went inside.

Phone Call

I finished my spelling list in no time.

I opened my science book.

The phone rang.

My mother answered it. "Sly, it's for you."

I went into the kitchen. My mother handed me an apple and the phone.

I took a bite. "Hello?" I said between chews.

"He did it again," said Melody.

"Is he doing it now?" I said.

"No."

"Were you playing catch when he started?" I said.

"Yes."

"Don't play catch," I said.

"Okay."

"And don't teach him to bite cats."

"We didn't use the stuffed cat," Melody yelped. "We never use it. I just brought it out today because we were in the house. We usually play catch with a ball. But my mother won't let me throw a ball in the house. So I was going to use the cat. Just that once," said Melody. "Stop saying I'm teaching Pong to bite cats. I'm not."

I waited to see if she was finished. "All right," I said.

"Bye," said Melody.

"Bye."

I looked out the window.

Brian was crawling again. This time he was in my yard.

That was my fault. I told him Wilson might have left his yard.

"Sly, come in here please," said Mother.

I went to Mother.

"Your first sentence makes no sense," said Mother. She held my spelling homework. "That's not how to use *evolve*."

"The dictionary said *evolve* means to develop," I said.

"It does mean that. But it usually means to develop over time—over a long time. Like how some small dinosaurs evolved into birds. And you can't evolve something else—things just evolve on their own."

"Oh," I said.

"Daddy doesn't develop his own pictures," said Mother.

"I just wanted to make an interesting sentence."

Dictionaries are dumb. They don't give enough information. And I just realized something: I needed more information.

Outside

I went outside.

"Hi, Brian."

"I can't find Wilson." Brian sat back on his heels. He looked sad. "Taxi is a murderer."

"You can't know that for sure."

"Watch." Brian jumped around like a madman.

He reminded me of something. I couldn't think what.

Taxi came from under the bushes. She sat on the stoop. She watched Brian.

"See?" said Brian. "Taxi wants to eat me."

Oh, now I got what all that jumping was. "You didn't look like Wilson, Brian."

"Maybe not to you."

Brian had a point. And he was becoming pathetic. "All right, Brian, tell you what. If you don't find Wilson by Saturday, I'll take my allowance and buy you a new mouse."

"I don't want a mouse," said Brian.

"Come on, Brian, all mice are the same."

"I know. That's why I don't want one."

There was no hope to this conversation. "See you later, Brian."

I walked into Brian's yard, through the rear hedges, and into Melody's yard.

I knocked on her back door.

Melody opened the door. She held Pong in her arms. He wiggled when he saw me.

"Where did you play catch with Pong?" I said.

"In the backyard," said Melody.

"Get the ball," I said.

"But you said not to play catch anymore."

"Just get the ball."

Monkey

Melody and Pong ran outside.

I followed.

"Let's play monkey in the middle," said Melody.

That sounded good to me. Melody throws fine. I throw even better. I play baseball, after all.

Melody threw me the ball.

Pong ran toward me and jumped.

I threw Melody the ball.

Pong ran back toward Melody and jumped.

Melody threw me the ball.

Pong ran toward me.

I threw Melody the ball.

Pong ran toward Melody.

Melody threw me the ball.

Pong threw himself on the ground. He panted.

Melody laughed.

I laughed.

Pong gave a breathless bark.

"He hates being the monkey," I said. "Just play catch with him, like you did before."

"Here, Pong." Melody threw the ball to Pong.

Pong lay there. The ball hit him in the face. He yipped.

"Oh, poor baby," said Melody. She ran to Pong and sat on the ground beside him. "You're so pooped, you can't move."

I sat down too. "Does he always get pooped so fast?"

"No. Usually he chases the ball a couple of times. Then he loses interest and wanders off. That's when the weird stuff starts."

"Have you got two bananas?" I said.

"I thought we were through with the monkey theme," said Melody. "Besides, Pong just licks bananas. He won't eat them."

"But we will. And we need something to eat while we wait."

"What are we waiting for?"

I was stalling. But Melody didn't need to know that. "Just get the bananas."

So Much Jumping Going On

We finished our bananas.

Pong was still recovering.

Finally, Pong got up. He wandered through the grass.

"Come back, Pong," said Melody.

"Shhh," I said. "Let him go. I need to see him act weird."

"But he might go through the hedge into Brian's yard."

"We can stop him if he tries," I said.

Melody frowned. But she didn't say anything else.

Pong wandered along.

Then he jumped.

"He's doing it," said Melody. She got to her feet.

I grabbed her hand and pulled her back down. "Wait."

Pong jumped in the other direction.

Pong jumped twice in a row.

He practically flipped over and jumped in the other direction.

He looked surprised.

And he reminded me of something.

He reminded me of Brian—when Brian was trying to act like Wilson.

And now I knew what Brian had reminded me of. He reminded me of Melody—when Melody had been trying to jump like Pong.

So much jumping going on.

And Brian didn't want a new mouse.

And his mother put Wilson in a bucket.

And, what had Brian said? Wilson would like ponds.

A Bucket

"Go get a bucket," I said.

"We can't put Pong in a bucket," said Melody.

"It's not for Pong. Get a deep one."

Melody ran into her garage. She brought back a beach bucket.

"Get ready," I said. "We're about to catch Wilson."

"Who's Wilson?"

"Brian's pet."

"Oh. What is he?"

I didn't know for sure. "You'll see. Come on."

I walked up behind Pong.

Pong jumped.

I snatched the little froggy in front of him. "Yay," I said, "we found Wilson." I dropped him in the bucket.

"Look," said Melody. She pointed.

Pong jumped again.

I caught another frog. "Wow."

Pong jumped.

Melody caught a frog. "Ack!" She dropped it in the grass. "Yuck, they're slimy."

"What did you expect?"

"How many are there?" said Melody.

"I don't know. Brian never told me there was more than one."

"I'll go call Jack. He's good at frogs," said Melody.

No More Tears

"Got him," said Jack. He put a frog in the bucket.

Pong jumped.

"Got him," said Jack. He put another frog in the bucket.

I put a frog in myself.

"Got him," said Jack.

I didn't know why Jack had to announce every frog he caught. But he was catching a lot. So it was okay.

Pong kept jumping.

Jack and I kept catching.

Finally, Pong stopped jumping.

We waited awhile.

Pong wandered.

Then he jumped.

Jack caught another frog.

We waited.

Melody's father drove into the driveway.

"Pong and I have to go inside now," said Melody.

"I'll stay awhile," said Jack. "Just to be sure."

"You solved the case," said Melody. "You can choose what baseball cards you want."

"Tomorrow." I picked up the bucket. "I'll bring these froggies to Brian now," I said.

Melody smiled and went inside.

I pushed my way through the hedge.

Brian sat in my driveway, looking sad.

When he saw the bucket in my hand, he smiled. Just like Melody.

"Here," I said. "Which one is Wilson?"

"They're all Wilson."

"You mean you named each one Wilson?"

"No, they're all Wilson. All together."

"You named all your frogs Wilson." I looked down into the bucket. "Well, is Wilson complete now?"

"Let's see. One, two, six, nine, twenty, sixteen. Yup. That's Wilson."

Frog Dog

My third case fit, after all. It was the case of the Frog Dog.

Pong loves to jump like Wilson. Just for fun, Melody brought over Pong yesterday and Brian put one part of Wilson into the grass. Pong jumped like crazy. We all laughed. And no frog was hurt.

Everyone was happy. Except Taxi. She hissed at Pong.

Pong hid behind Melody.

Pong is a funny dog.

And that concludes my three pet cases. Each case was a success.

It's great being Sly the Sleuth.